American Holidays / Celebraciones en los Estados Unidos

PRESIDENTS' DAY
DÍA DE LOS PRESIDENTES

Connor Dayton Traducción al español: Eduardo Alamán

PowerKiDS
press™

New York

Published in 2012 by The Rosen Publishing Group, Inc.
29 East 21st Street, New York, NY 10010

First Edition

Editor: Jennifer Way
Book Design: Julio Gil

Traducción al español: Eduardo Alamán

Photo Credits: Cover (crowd) Ryan Rodrick Beiler/Shutterstock.com; cover (background) Medioimages/Photodisc/Thinkstock; p. 5 Christopher Penler/Shutterstock.com; p. 7 Universal History Archive/Getty Images; p. 9 SuperStock/Getty Images; p. 11 Michael Kovac/WireImage/Getty Images; pp. 13, 17, 19, 21, 24 (top right, top left) Shutterstock.com; pp. 14–15, 24 (bottom) Wendy Connett/Robert Harding World Imagery/Getty Images; p. 23 Mark Ralston/AFP/Getty Images.

Library of Congress Cataloging-in-Publication Data

Dayton, Connor.
  [Presidents' Day. Spanish & English]
  Presidents' Day = Día de los Presidentes / by Connor Dayton. — 1st ed.
      p. cm. — (American holidays = Celebraciones en los Estados Unidos)
  Includes index.
  ISBN 978-1-4488-6708-0 (library binding)
  1. Presidents' Day—Juvenile literature. 2. Presidents—United States—History—Juvenile literature. I. Title.
  II. Title: Día de los Presidentes.
  E176.8.D3918 2012
  394.261—dc23

                                    2011024153

Web Sites: Due to the changing nature of Internet links, PowerKids Press has developed an online list of Web sites related to the subject of this book. This site is updated regularly. Please use this link to access the list: www.powerkidslinks.com/amh/president/

Manufactured in the United States of America

CPSIA Compliance Information: Batch #WW12PK: For Further Information contact Rosen Publishing, New York, New York at 1-800-237-9932

Contents

Contenido

Presidents' Day is the third
Monday in February.

El Día de los Presidentes
se celebra el tercer lunes
de febrero.

Washington's Birthday is the real name for this holiday. George Washington was born on February 22, 1732.

El nombre real de esta celebración es Natalicio de George Washington. Washington nació el 22 de febrero de 1732.

Presidents' Day also honors Abraham Lincoln. Lincoln was born on February 12, 1809.

El Día de los Presidentes también honra a Abraham Lincoln. Lincoln nació el 12 de febrero de 1809.

Presidents' Day can honor all of America's presidents.

El Día de los Presidentes celebra a todos los presidentes de los Estados Unidos.

Presidents' Day is a day to learn about America.

El Día de los Presidentes es un día para aprender sobre los Estados Unidos.

The president lives and works in the **White House**. It is in Washington, D.C.

El presidente vive y trabaja en la **Casa Blanca**. Ésta se encuentra en Washington, D.C.

The Washington **Monument** is the tallest building in Washington, D.C.

El **Monumento** a Washington es el edificio más alto de Washington, D.C.

The Lincoln **Memorial** is also in Washington, D.C. Lincoln is America's tallest president.

El monumento **conmemorativo** a Lincoln también está en Washington D.C. Lincoln es el presidente más alto de los Estados Unidos.

Mount Rushmore shows four American presidents. It is in South Dakota.

El Monte Rushmore muestra cuatro presidentes de los Estados Unidos. Se encuentra en Dakota del Sur.

What do you do on
Presidents' Day?

¿Qué haces tú el Día de
los Presidentes?

Words to Know / Palabras que debes saber

memorial
(el monumento) conmemorativo

monument / (el) monumento

White House / (la) Casa Blanca

Index

Índice